# The World of ARTHUR

# and Friends

## MARC BROWN

LITTLE, BROWN AND COMPANY

New York ❧ Boston

Little, Brown and Company

Time Warner Book Group
1271 Avenue of the Americas, New York, NY 10020
Visit our Web site at www.lb-kids.com

First Edition

Arthur® is a registered trademark of Marc Brown.

*Arthur's Teacher Moves In*: LCCN 99-043720
*Arthur's Underwear*: LCCN 99-025702
*Arthur Lost and Found*: LCCN 97-46992
*Arthur's Computer Disaster*: LCCN 96-42418
*Arthur Writes a Story*: LCCN 95-43201
*Arthur's TV Trouble*: LCCN 94-48816

LCCN 2004106349
ISBN 0-316-01045-6

10 9 8 7 6 5 4 3 2 1

PHX

Printed in the United States of America

# Contents

It was Friday afternoon, and Arthur was relaxing.
"Whew. . . no Mr. Ratburn all weekend,"
Arthur said.
"Arthur," said Mom. "I just heard some bad news. The snow collapsed Mr. Ratburn's roof, and he has nowhere to stay."

"Oh, too bad,"
Arthur said, his
eyes glued to the TV.
"I knew you'd feel
that way," his
mother said. "So
we invited him to
stay here."
"Oh, okay,"
Arthur said, still
watching TV.

"Stay HERE???"
Arthur ran after
Mom.

"Mom—what did—you—he—where is—*what did you say?*"
Arthur stammered.
"Arthur's teacher's going to stay here!" sang D.W.
"Just until his roof is fixed," said his mother.
Arthur couldn't believe it.

Later that day, Arthur told Buster the news.
"It's too weird," Arthur said. "My teacher in my house, walking on
my carpet, eating from my spoons and touching my stuff!"
Buster agreed. "School is at school and home is at home because
that's the way it's supposed to be."
"Exactly!" Arthur nodded.

But his parents didn't understand.

"It's just plain wrong," Arthur tried to explain. "It goes against nature!"

"The poor man has nowhere else to go," said Dad.

"He's going to stay here," said Mom, "and we're *all* going to make him feel welcome."

Arthur tried to imagine
Mr. Ratburn staying at his
house, but the picture in his
head was too horrible.

The next day, Arthur borrowed books from the Brain and rushed home to put up new posters.

"Why are you putting a poster on top of another poster?" asked D.W.

"You wouldn't understand," Arthur answered.

"Are you trying to make Mr. Ragworm think you're smarter than you really are?"

"Go away," Arthur said.

Then the doorbell rang.

"Arthur! D.W.!" Mom called. "Come say hello!"

"Hi, Mr. Ratbite," said D.W. "Is it true that you torture kids?"

"Here I am!" Arthur cried. "Welcome! Hello! Come in!"

"Please take these up to your room, Arthur," said Dad.

"He's staying in Arthur's room!" sang D.W.

"I put your sleeping bag in D.W.'s room," said Mom.

"Hey, no fair!" said D.W.

Mr. Ratburn saw the books on Arthur's table.

"Those are my favorite books in the whole world," Arthur said.

"Hmmm," Mr. Ratburn said. "*Trigonometry for Fun… The Double Helix and You…*"

"Didn't you just borrow those from the Brain?" said D.W.

"I use my *brain* a lot," Arthur said quickly.

"Mr. Ropeburns," said D.W., "look what's under here..."
Arthur quickly leaned against the poster. "I think I smell Dad
making a cake," he said.
"Cake!" said D.W.  She ran out the door.
"Cake?" said Mr. Ratburn. He ran out, too.
Arthur sank onto his bed, relieved.

Later, Arthur was watching *The Bionic Bunny Show.* But when Mr. Ratburn came into the room, Arthur quickly changed the channel.

"You look … different," Arthur said.

"I don't always dress for school," said Mr. Ratburn.

"Mr. Rathead," said D.W., "you were lucky you weren't in school when the roof fell in."
"It was the roof to my home," said Mr. Ratburn.
D.W. looked confused. "Teachers don't live at school," Mr. Ratburn explained. "We have houses just like you do."
"Oh," said D.W. "The world was so simple until now."

"Would you might like to watch one of my videos?" Mr. Ratburn asked Arthur.

"Of course," said Arthur. "I *love* educational videos."

A cartoon kangaroo appeared on the screen.

"*Spooky Poo?*" Arthur said.

"One of my favorites!" said Mr. Ratburn.

After *Spooky Poo*, Mr. Ratburn covered up Arthur's history book
with a handkerchief and waved his hand over it.
When he pulled the handkerchief away, the book was gone!
"Shazam! No homework tonight!"
"Wow!" said Arthur. "Can you teach me that?"
"Sure," Mr. Ratburn said.

For dessert, Dad
brought out a
huge cake.

"I like it when Mr. Ragburp stays with us," said D.W.

On Monday morning, Arthur's friends all shook their heads.
"Can you imagine Ratburn living with you?" said Buster.
"I bet Arthur's ready to run away," said Francine.
"Hey, Arthur," said Buster, "you can stay at my house until Ratburn goes home."
"It's not so bad," said Arthur. "He taught me a magic trick. We had fun."
Mr. Ratburn waved at Arthur. Arthur waved back.

At lunch, everyone was talking about the math test.

"I got a C minus," Buster said.

"You beat me," Muffy said.

"Arthur got an A," said Francine. "It's not fair!"

"Yeah, *we* could all get A's if Mr. Ratburn lived with *us* and *our* fathers made cakes for him," said Muffy.

"But I studied hard for that test!" Arthur protested.

"Sure you did," everyone said.

After school, all of Arthur's friends were busy.
"Want to watch some *Spooky Poo*?" Arthur asked.
"I don't think so," said Buster. "I don't want to get between you and
your new *friend*."

"Want to go to the Sugar Bowl for some hot cocoa?" Arthur asked
Francine and Muffy.
Francine shook her head. "Sorry. We're already going to the Sugar
Bowl for some hot cocoa."

Then the Brain asked for his books back.
"Sure," said Arthur. "I'll bring them to your house."
"No, thanks. Please bring them to school," said the Brain.

"Teacher's pet, teacher's pet," sang Binky. "That means you, Arthur!"
Then he handed Arthur a note from Fern.
Arthur walked home alone.

Pal was at the door
to greet him.
"It's great to get
home," said Arthur,
"and forget all about
school."

Mr. Ratburn was at the kitchen table, eating cake. "Oh," said Arthur. "Hi." He quickly left the room.

Later, Arthur showed Fern's drawing to his parents and Mr. Ratburn. "And Binky called me a 'teacher's pet,'" Arthur said.
"Maybe I should talk to everyone," said Mr.Ratburn.
"No!" Arthur said. "That will make it worse!"

"You know I wouldn't give you special treatment," Mr. Ratburn said. "And you *have* studied hard lately." "If you give me an F," said Arthur, "that'll prove I'm not a teacher's pet." "Soon they'll realize that they're wrong," said Mom. "Not as soon as if he gave me an F," said Arthur sadly.

Tuesday at lunch, everyone made fun of Arthur.

"Teacher's pet, teacher's pet," sang Binky.

"If cake gets you one A, will apple pie get you two A's?" said Francine.

"Maybe with some vanilla ice cream on top," said Muffy.

Arthur tried to laugh.

Mr. Ratburn walked over.

"Arthur, I won't be staying at your house anymore."

"Really?" said Arthur.

Mr. Ratburn nodded.

"I need to be closer to my house to supervise the work on the roof, so…"

Francine's parents have invited me to stay with them. After that, I'll be staying at Binky's house. Who knows?" said Mr. Ratburn as he walked away. "I may also stay at Muffy's, Buster's, Fern's…"

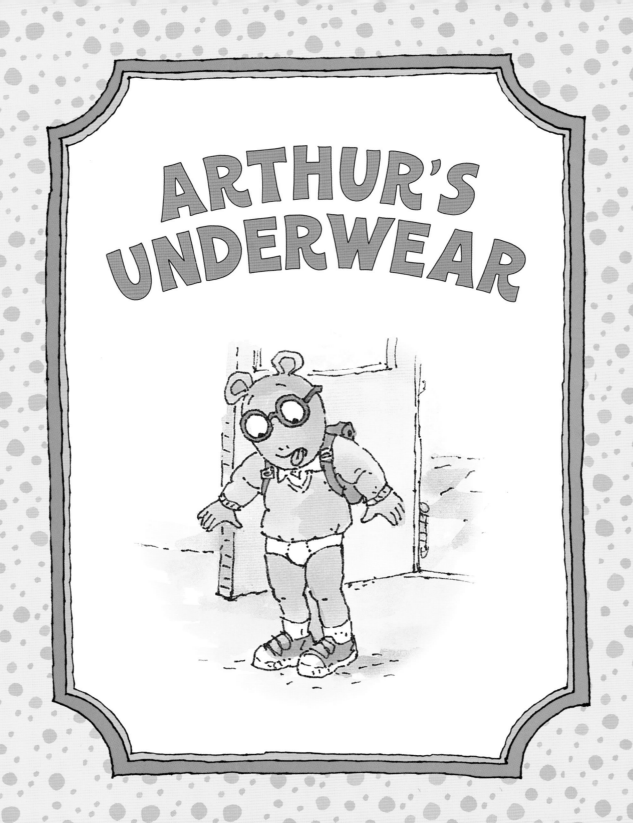

Binky was at the board doing a difficult problem.
"That's correct," said Mr. Ratburn. "Very good."

Binky cheered, "Yes!" and dropped his chalk. As he bent down, the class heard a loud *RRRIPPP!*

Everyone laughed, except Mr. Ratburn. "Go to the office and ask Ms. Tingley to sew them up," he said.

That afternoon at softball practice, when Binky came up to bat,
Arthur thought about Binky in his underwear and laughed.
During dinner, Mom asked, "Anything interesting happen at
school today?"
Arthur started to laugh.
"What's so funny?" asked D.W.
But Arthur couldn't stop laughing to answer.

The next morning, Arthur woke up late.
He hurried through breakfast and ran most of the way to school.
"Sorry I'm late, Mr. Ratburn! I guess my alarm—"
Everyone burst out laughing.
"Mr. Read, being late is one thing,"
said Mr. Ratburn,
"but not wearing
any trousers—
*that* is quite
another!"
Arthur looked
down—and
screamed!

Arthur's scream woke him up.
*Wow*, he thought, *what a horrible dream!*

In school, the class watched a science film. "The amoeba is a single-celled life form..."
Arthur's eyelids began to droop.

Suddenly, an amoeba that looked a lot like Arthur appeared on the screen. Its pants fell down, showing its underwear.

"Help!" cried Arthur-Amoeba. "I need my pants!"
All the other amoebas started to laugh.

Arthur-Amoeba was too embarrassed to move. Then he felt
someone shaking him.
"Wake up, Arthur!" said Buster. "The movie's over."

At lunch, Arthur didn't feel like eating.
"What should I do, Buster? Every time I go to sleep, I'm in my underwear!"
"Try staying awake," Buster suggested. "You can't dream if you don't sleep."

That night, Arthur tried some tricks to stay awake.

Old MacDonald had a farm...

But as hard as he tried,
Arthur just couldn't.

"I'll get you, Verminator…. After… I take… a little nap."

In Arthur's dream, the Verminator was torturing the class by scratching his claws on the blackboard. Hearing cries for help, Bionic Arthur rushed to the rescue!

But as he entered the classroom to take on the Verminator, everyone started laughing.

"My pants!" Arthur gasped as he woke up with a start.
"Rise and shine, Mr. Fancy Pants," said D.W. "They're right here. Mom says you better shake a leg or you'll be late for school!"

Arthur asked Buster for some emergency advice on
the way to school.

"It even happens when I'm a superhero!" he
exclaimed. "I can't stay awake forever. I'm doomed!"

"Maybe you should sleep in your pants," said Buster.
"That way you don't have to worry about putting
them on."

That night,
D.W. came into
Arthur's room.
"Why are you
wearing your
pants to bed?"
she asked.
"Because ... ah ...
that way I can be
ready for school
faster," he said
quickly.

"I'm going to ask
Mom if I can sleep
in my clothes too,"
D.W. said. "And
maybe my coat
and boots.
*Mom?!*"
Arthur sighed and
changed into his
pajama pants.

The next day, Arthur was more worried than ever. "What if people find out about my underwear problem?" he asked Buster. "They'll call me names, and then I'll have to change schools…"
"Don't worry," said Buster. "Your secret is safe with me."

At lunch the following day, Arthur sat with Francine and Muffy. They looked at him and started to giggle.

"What's so funny?" Arthur asked.

"Do you have your pants on?" asked Francine. "Better make sure!"

Arthur checked. He *was* wearing pants.

He moved to another table.

"I heard about your nightmares," said the Brain, "so I got out a couple of books on dreams. Apparently, you have a pathological fear of embarrassment…"

Arthur got up to find Buster.

"Buster!" cried Arthur. "You told everyone about my underwear dreams!"

"Not everyone," replied Buster. "Only a few kids."

"Buster, how could you?"

"Well, I couldn't help you. I needed some advice."

"This is so embarrassing!" said Arthur.

When Arthur turned to run out of the cafeteria, his pants pocket got caught.
*RRRIPPP!*

Everyone in the cafeteria began to laugh.
Arthur couldn't move.
But Binky quickly grabbed two trays to cover him.
"Quick!" he whispered. "Into the kitchen!"

Mrs. MacGrady wrapped her apron around Arthur and got out a needle and thread.

"I'm sorry," Buster said. "I shouldn't have told anyone."

"It's okay," said Arthur sadly. "You were just trying to help. The hard part will be telling my parents that I have to change schools."

Mrs. MacGrady handed Arthur his pants.

"Thanks," said Arthur. "Is there a back door?"

"Afraid not," said Mrs. MacGrady. "But do you know the old saying, 'A banana without its peel is still a banana'?"

"Huh?" said Arthur and Buster.

"It means people get embarrassed all the time," Binky explained.

"But you're still Arthur," said Mrs. MacGrady. "A smart, kind young man—with or without your pants."

Arthur smiled.

A few days later, Arthur met Buster at the Sugar Bowl.
"Well, no more underwear nightmares!" Arthur said.
"That's great!" said Buster. "I never thought that ripping your pants in the cafeteria would be the thing to cure you."
As they stood up to leave, Arthur looked at Buster and frowned.
"Uh, Buster… I think you forgot something."

Buster woke up with a scream.
"Uh-oh," he sighed. "Here we go again!"

"What are you supposed to be?" asked Arthur.
"I'm mashed potatoes," said D.W., "in the Festival of Foods at school tomorrow."

"Gee, too bad I have my swimming
lesson," said Arthur.
"You'll have to take the bus to your
lesson," said Mom, "and I'll pick
you up."
"All by myself?" asked Arthur.
"We've taken the bus before," said
Mom. "You know how."
"Maybe I'll ask Buster to come
along," said Arthur.
"Good idea," said Mom.

On the way to school, Arthur invited Buster.

"You mean the real bus?" asked Buster. "The one that goes all the way to the end of town?"

"Sure," said Arthur. "We just pay our money and go."

"I don't know," said Buster. "I heard about this guy who got on the bus, and it just kept going and going."

"We can study for our science test, and you can watch me swim," said Arthur. "It'll be fun."

After school,
Arthur and Buster
waited at the
bus stop.
"Did you hear
about the kid who
didn't have enough
money?" asked
Francine. "The
driver wouldn't let
him off the bus."

All of a sudden Arthur didn't feel so well. "Here comes the bus!" said Francine. "Good luck."

"Exact change only," growled the driver.

The boys paid him and quickly took their seats.

"Want to study for the test?" asked Arthur.

"Not really," said Buster.

Arthur took out his science book.

"'Chapter six,'" read Arthur. "'Habits of the Clam...'"

By the time the bus stopped, Arthur and Buster were
sound asleep.

"Last stop," called the driver. "Everyone out!"

"Where are we?" asked Arthur.

"Who knows?" said Buster. "I think we passed the pool."

"I've never seen this part of town before," said Buster.
"We're lost!"
"Maybe we can find a police officer," said Arthur.

"Wait!" said Arthur. "There's a place with a phone!"

But the telephone had a sign on it.
"Sorry, it's been broken for weeks,"
said the man behind the counter.
"I'm hungry," said Buster. "I always
get hungry when I'm scared."
"No, you're just always hungry,"
said Arthur.
They bought six chocolate Winkies
and two cans of strawberry soda and
thought about what to do next.

Meanwhile, back at home, the phone rang.

D.W. ran to answer it.

"Mom," D.W. yelled, "did we lose Arthur somewhere?"

"He's at his swimming lesson," said Mom. "In fact, it's almost time to pick him up. Who is it?"

"It's the man from the pool," said D.W. "Arthur isn't there."

"Give me the phone," gasped Mom. "What do you mean he's not there?"

"If Arthur's lost," said D.W., "can I have his room?"

Arthur and Buster finished their snacks. Then Arthur got an idea.
"Let's go back to the bus stop and try to get a bus home," said Arthur.
"Great idea!" said Buster. "Can you loan me some money for the bus?
I spent all my money on Winkies."
"Sure," said Arthur.
But when Arthur reached into his pocket, it was empty.
"Oh no," said Arthur. "I spent all my money on strawberry sodas!"
"We're doomed," said Buster.
"Let's go to the bus stop anyway," said Arthur. "Maybe we can talk
to the bus driver."

Arthur and Buster raced to the bus stop.
The bus was just pulling away.
"Oh no!" said Arthur. "Wait! WAIT!" he called.
The bus squealed to a stop.
"Whaddaya kids want?" asked the driver.
"We're lost," Arthur explained.

"We were supposed to get off at the pool, but we fell asleep and then we spent all of our money on Winkies. Now we can't get home, and I'm really sorry."

"Hey, kids," said the driver, "I've heard enough. Happens all the time."

"Really?" asked Arthur.

"Hop on," said the driver. "By the way, my name's Sam."

"I'm Arthur. He's Buster."

"Let's make a quick stop and give your folks a call," said Sam. "Just in case they're getting a little nervous."

"Great idea," said Arthur.

Sam stopped the bus right in front of Arthur's house instead of the corner.

"Thanks, Sam," said Arthur and Buster.

"See ya 'round," said Sam.

Everyone on the bus waved good-bye.

When Arthur
opened the door,
his family ran to
give him kisses
and hugs.
D.W. was so happy
that she hugged
Buster, too.
"No kisses, please,"
said Buster.
Arthur told his
family everything
that had happened.

"I liked the part
where you were
lost best," said
D.W.
"That's when I had
a new bedroom."
Then Dad gave
Buster a ride
home.

That night, when both Mom and Dad had tucked Arthur into bed, he was very sleepy.
"You were smart to figure out what to do," said Mom.
"We're very proud of you," said Dad.
They kissed Arthur good night and turned off the light.

Suddenly, the door burst open and the light went on.
"What's going on?" said Arthur.
"I'm making sure you're not lost again," said D.W.
"Good brothers are hard to find."
Arthur yawned. "So are good sisters.
Good night, D.W."

"Mom, can I use your computer to play *Deep, Dark Sea*?" asked Arthur.

"What's *Deep, Dark Sea*?" asked D.W.

"Only the greatest game in the universe," said Arthur. "Can I, Mom, please?"

"What's the game about?" asked D.W. "A haunted sunken ship," said Arthur. "With skeletons, ghosts, and sharks." "Sounds spooky," said D.W.

"Mom, please," begged Arthur. "Oh, all right," said Mom, "but finish your dinner first."

Arthur finished his dinner in a jiffy.

Once Arthur
started playing
*Deep, Dark Sea*,
he couldn't stop.
"Time for bed,"
said Dad.
"But Dad, I almost
found *the thing*,"
said Arthur.

"When I find *the thing*, I can win stuff."

"You can find *the thing* tomorrow," said Dad. "It's bedtime."

"I'm ready for bed," said D.W. sweetly.

The next morning, Buster came over to play *Deep, Dark Sea*. "Sorry, boys," said Mom. "It's tax season. I need my computer all day."

Just then the phone rang. It was for Mom. "I have to run to the office," she said. "And don't touch my computer."

After Mom left, Arthur and Buster stared at the computer.

"I know what you're thinking," said D.W.

"But I'm so close to finding *the thing*," said Arthur.

"You could probably find it before your mom gets home," said Buster.

"I'm telling Dad," warned D.W.

"I'll give you my desserts for a whole week," said Arthur.

"And play dollhouse with me whenever I say so?" asked D.W.

"Yes," grumbled Arthur.

"And call me Your Royal Highness . . .?" asked D.W.

"Don't push it," said Arthur.

Arthur loaded the
game.
"Look out for the
Squid Squad!" yelled
Buster.
"I'm running out of
oxygen," said
Arthur.
"Look," said Buster.
"A treasure chest!"

"That's it!"
screamed Arthur.
"That's *the thing*! I
found it!"
"Let me open it!"
shouted Buster.
"I found it," argued
Arthur.
They both dove for
the mouse.

The keyboard crashed to the floor.
"Uh-oh," said Arthur.
"You're in big trouble," said D.W.

Just then the phone rang. Everyone jumped.
It was Mom.
"I won't be home until tonight," she said. "Everything all right?"
"Umm, fine, just great," said Arthur.
"You know, Mom can tell when you're lying," whispered D.W.
"Maybe we can fix it before she gets home," said Arthur.

Arthur looked through the computer manual. "There's nothing in here about *Deep, Dark Sea* accidents," he said.

"Are you sure you have the right manual?" asked D.W.

"The Brain can fix anything," said Buster.
"Let's ask him."
"Alan's not home," said the Brain's mom.

They checked the library.

They checked the museum.
Just when they were about to give up, they found him.

"Are you doing a science experiment?" asked Buster.
"No, I'm skipping stones," said the Brain. "It's fun!"

Everyone went back to Arthur's house.

The Brain examined the computer.

"Hmmm," said the Brain. He shook his head.

"That bad?" asked Arthur.

"It must be," said the Brain. "I can't find the problem."

"Well, thanks for trying," said Arthur.

"Now you're in really, really big trouble," said D.W.

"If the Brain can't fix it, who can?" said Buster.

"I have an idea," said Arthur.

Arthur explained his problem to the computer expert.
Then the computer expert explained how much a house call and hourly fees would cost. "That's more birthday money than I'll ever see in my whole life," said Arthur. "I'm doomed."

"We're all doomed," said D.W. "Because now Mommy will lose her job and we won't be able to keep our house and we'll all have to live in the cold on the street and we'll all get ammonia and probably die and it's all your fault, Arthur!"

That evening,
Arthur hardly
touched his dinner.
"Hi, I'm home,"
called Mom.
"Mom, how about
a game of cards?"
asked Arthur.
"And a family
bike ride?"

"I don't have time, sweetie," said Mom. "I have tons of work."
Mom headed for the computer. Arthur felt sick.

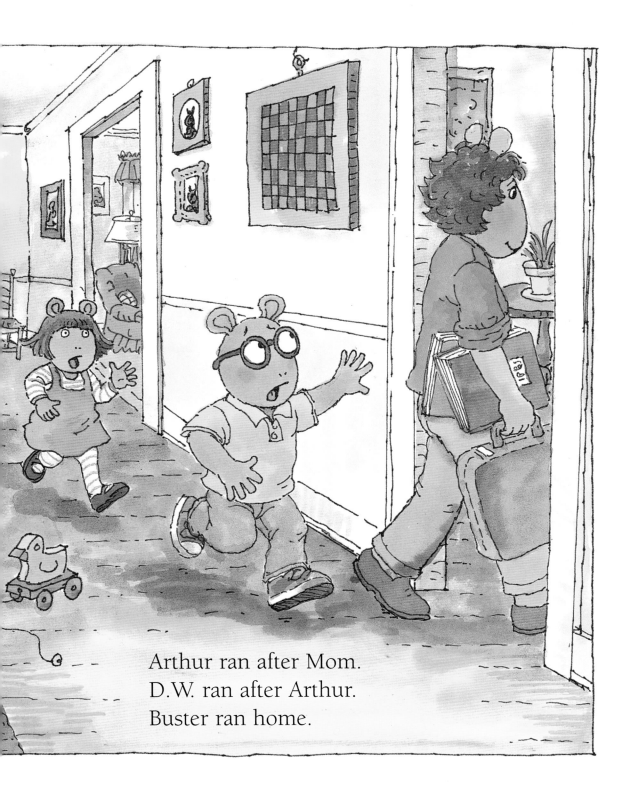

Arthur ran after Mom.
D.W. ran after Arthur.
Buster ran home.

Just as Mom's finger was about to hit the ON button,
Arthur yelled, "Stop!" He went on,
"I was playing *Deep, Dark Sea*, and the screen
went blank. I'm sorry. I wrecked it.
It's all my fault."

"That happens to me all
the time," said Mom.
"Did you jiggle the switch?"
Mom jiggled the switch, and
the game came on.
"Why didn't you call me?" asked Mom.
"Always call me with your problems."
"I thought you'd be mad," said Arthur.
"I'm not mad," said Mom. "I'm disappointed."

"Am I going to get punished?" asked Arthur.

"Of course," said Mom. "You did something you weren't supposed to do."

"Make the punishment really good," said D.W.

"No computer games for a week," said Mom. "Now, get ready for bed. I'll be up to say good night in a few minutes."

Arthur and D.W. did as they were told.
Then they waited for what seemed like a very
long time.

"Mom," called Arthur. "Time to tuck us in."

"In a minute," said Mom. "The sharks are
attacking!"

"Maybe we should tuck ourselves in tonight,"
said D.W.

"Good idea," said Arthur.

"I'll be right up," called Mom. "As soon as I blast these skeletons from the treasure chest."

"Good night, Mom," called D.W.
"Good night, Mom," called Arthur.

# ARTHUR
## WRITES A STORY

Arthur's teacher, Mr. Ratburn, explained the homework.
"What should the story be about?" Arthur asked.
"Anything," Mr. Ratburn said. "Write about something that is important to you."

Arthur started his story the minute he got home. He knew exactly what he wanted to write about.

# How I Got My Puppy Pal

I always wanted a dog, but first I had to prove I was responsible. So I started Arthur's Pet Business. My mom made me keep all the animals in the basement. It was a lot of work, but it was fun until I thought I lost Perky. But then I found her, and she had three puppies! And I got to keep one of them. That's how I got my dog Pal.

The End

Arthur read his story to D.W. "That's a boring story," D.W. said. "Does it have to be real life? Because your life is so dull."

"I don't want to write a boring story," said Arthur. "If it were me," D.W. suggested, "I'd make the story about getting an elephant."

The next day, Arthur read his new story to Buster.

"Did you like the part about the elephant puppies?" he asked.
"It's okay, I guess," said Buster. "I'm writing a cool story about outer space."

*Maybe my story should take place on the moon,* thought Arthur.

On Wednesday, Arthur read his newest story to the Brain. "Scientifically speaking, elephants would weigh less on the moon, but wouldn't float that high," said the Brain.

"So you don't like it?" asked Arthur. "A good story should be well researched," said the Brain. "Like mine: 'If I Had A Pet Stegosaurus in the Jurassic Period.'"

Arthur hurried to the library.

"What are all those books for?" asked Francine.

"Research," said Arthur. "I'm writing about my pet five-toed mammal of the genus *Loxodonta*."

"Your *what*?" asked Francine.

"My elephant!" Arthur explained.

"Oh," said Francine. "I'm putting jokes in my story."

All through dinner,
Arthur worried about
his story.
"Please pass the
corn," asked Father.

"Corn! That's it!" said Arthur. "Purple corn and blue elephants! On Planet Shmellafint! Now *that's* funny."
"Arthur is acting weirder than usual," said D.W.

On Thursday, everyone at the Sugar Bowl was talking about their stories.

"Last year, a kid wrote a country-western song for her story," said Prunella. "And she got an A$^+$."

"How do you know?" asked Arthur.
"That kid was me," explained Prunella. "Mr. Ratburn said I should send it to a record company. It was *that* good."
"Wow!" said Arthur.

That night, Arthur's
imagination went wild.

He decided to turn his story into a song. He even made up a dance to go with it.

Later, he tried it out on his family.
"…Now this little boy
Can go home and enjoy
His own personal striped elephant.
And you will see
How happy he will be
Here on Planet…
Shmellafint!"

"Well," said Arthur. "What do you think?"

Mother and Father smiled.
"It's nice," said Grandma Thora.
"But a little confusing."
"Too bad you can't dance," said D.W.

"What am I going to do?" said Arthur. "My story is due tomorrow." That night Arthur didn't sleep very well.

The next day,
Arthur worried
until Mr. Ratburn
finally called on
him.

When Arthur's song and dance was over, the classroom was so quiet, it was almost spooky. Binky raised his hand.
"Did that really happen?"

"Sort of," said Arthur. "It started as the story of how I got my dog."
"I'd like to hear that story," said Mr. Ratburn.

"The title was 'How I Got My Puppy Pal,'" said Arthur.
Arthur told how proud he was of his pet business and how scared he was when Perky disappeared. And he told how happy he was to find her under his bed and how surprised he was to see her three puppies. "And the best part is," said Arthur, "I got to keep one!"

Buster said, "I like that story better than your other one."

"Great story!" said Binky.

"I think Arthur's story was the best!" said Muffy.

166

"Good work," said Mr. Ratburn. "Of course, I expect you to write it all down by Monday."
Then Mr. Ratburn gave Arthur a gold sticker. "Oh, and one more thing," he said.

"Leave out the dancing!"

It all started when Arthur was watching
*The Bionic Bunny Show.*

"Dogs love 'em," said the announcer. "The amazing Treat Timer. Treat your pet to Treat Timer. Only $19.95. Treats may vary. Batteries not included. If you love your pet—get a Treat Timer!"

"Wow!" said Arthur. "Pal needs one of those."

Ads for the Treat Timer were everywhere.

Now Arthur really wanted one.

Arthur counted his money. D.W. helped.
"Even with all of my birthday money," he said,
"I only have ten dollars and three cents."
"I know what you're thinking," said D.W.
She ran to protect her cash register.

Arthur decided to ask Dad for an advance on his allowance. "Gee, I'd love to help," said Dad, "but my catering business is a little slow right now."

Arthur knew Mom would understand.

"Money doesn't grow on trees," said Mother, "and I think Pal likes treats from you, not a machine."

On the way to school, Arthur was walking very slowly. "What are you doing?" asked Buster.

"Looking for money," said Arthur. "I want to buy Pal a Treat Timer."

"Those are very expensive," said Buster. "You need a job."

"I need a miracle," said Arthur.

At school, while everyone else took a spelling test, Arthur daydreamed about the Treat Timer.

Mr. Ratburn asked
Arthur to stay after
school to take the
test over.

Arthur took the long way home so he could think of a good excuse why he was late. Mr. Sipple was cleaning his garage.

"Hi, Arthur," he said. "Every fifty years I clean the place out. I could use a little help." "I could use a little money," said Arthur.

"All the newspapers need to be recycled," said Mr. Sipple.
"I'll pay you fifty cents to take them out to the curb."
"Great!" said Arthur. "I'll do it tomorrow."
"I won't be home until after dinner," said Mr. Sipple, "but you can get started. Everything you need to do the job is here."

*I'm rich!* thought Arthur.
All of a sudden, Arthur was in a big hurry to get home.

"I've got a job!" cried Arthur. "Now I can buy a Treat Timer!"

"Can I go to the mall with you?" asked D.W.

"Sure," said Arthur.

"I wish you were rich all the time," said D.W. "You're much nicer."

The next day, Arthur counted the stacks as he pulled them to the curb. Twenty-four.

"That makes twelve whole dollars!" cried Arthur. "I'll come back later to collect!"

"You look
exhausted," said
D.W. when Arthur
got home.
"I don't want to
see another
newspaper for a
long, long time,"
said Arthur.

"Well, then don't look out the window," said D.W.
"So that's what the string was for!" said Arthur.
"I'd better hurry before Mr. Sipple gets home."
"Wait for me," said D.W.

"You're in big trouble," said D.W.

"You missed some over there."

"These stacks are a lot neater."

"Are you using double knots?"

"Nice work!" said Mr. Sipple when he got home. "Here's your twelve dollars."

"Thank you, sir," said Arthur.

"I helped," said D.W. "Don't I get something?"

"You get a trip to the mall, remember?" said Arthur.

The next morning, Arthur and his family were the first ones at the mall. Arthur put his money on the counter. "One Treat Timer, please," he said.

"It looks bigger on TV," said Arthur when he saw the box. "You assemble it, of course," said the salesperson. "And remember, all sales are final."

Five hours later, the Treat Timer was assembled. "You're going to love it, Pal," said Arthur.

Pal sniffed it.
Arthur turned it
on. It clicked.
Lights flashed.

Treats shot out
like rockets.
Pal let out a
loud bark and ran
for cover. "Turn it
off!" yelled
Mother.

"I'm trying to," said Arthur. "But I think it's broken." "And remember," said D.W., "all sales are final." Arthur went to his room alone.

"I'm worried," said Mother. "He's been up there for hours."

"I know how to get him out," said D.W.

"It's seven o'clock," she yelled up the stairs. "*The Bionic Bunny Show* is on!"

Seconds later, Arthur appeared.

"Sit down," said D.W., "so I can protect you from those nasty commercials."

"I don't need these!" said Arthur. "There's no way a TV ad will get my hard-earned money again."

"It's the Magic Disappearing Box!" said the announcer. "Astound your friends! Eliminate your enemies! The Magic Disappearing Box from KidTricks!"

"Hmmm," said Arthur. "Now this could be useful."

"What would you ever do with that?" asked D.W.

Marc Brown's

# ARTHUR ADVENTURES

Read Them All!

**Marc Brown** is the creator of the bestselling Arthur Adventure book series and co-developer of the Emmy Award–winning PBS television series, *Arthur*. He has also created a second book series, featuring D.W., Arthur's little sister, as well as numerous other books for children. Marc Brown lives with his family in Hingham, Massachusetts, and on Martha's Vineyard.